This Little Tiger book belongs to:

_____

_____

_____

For Olaf, with love
- Gaby Hansen

LITTLE TIGER PRESS
I The Coda Centre, 189 Munster Road, London SW6 6AW
www.littletiger.co.uk

First published in Great Britain 2002
This edition published 2016

Ready for Bed!

Jane Johnson
illustrated by Gaby Hansen

LITTLE TIGER PRESS
London

"Aaah, peace and quiet at last," sighed Mrs Rabbit.
"All my children are tucked up safe in bed."

But Mrs Rabbit had spoken too soon!

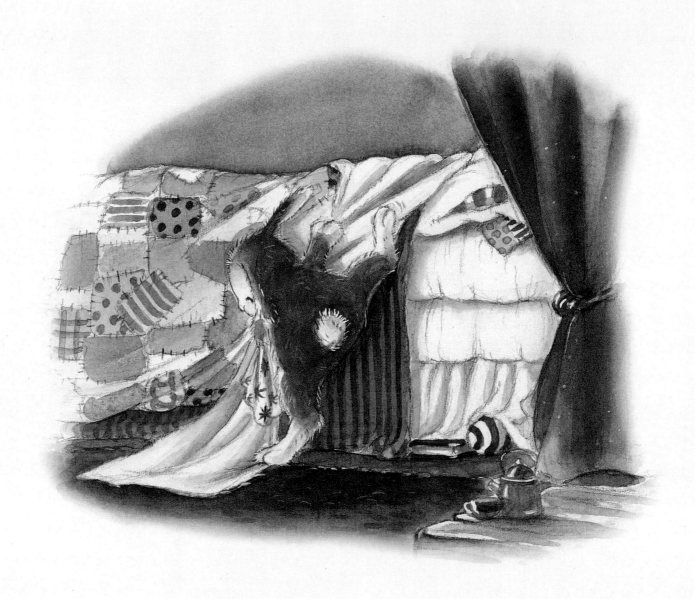

"I can't sleep, Mummy," said her youngest
little bunny, interrupting her first snore.

Mrs Rabbit tried a gentle lullaby.
"Hush-a-bye bunny on the treetop,
when the bough bends, the cradle . . ."
Little Bunny's eyes began to close.
"Is my bunny sleepy now?" whispered
Mrs Rabbit, so as not to wake the others.

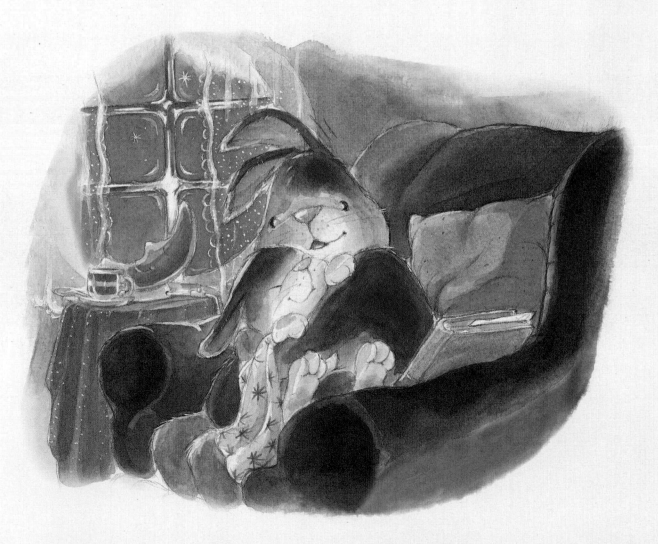

"No!" said Little Bunny. "Not at all sleepy."
He wanted his mummy all to himself.

Mrs Rabbit tried a bubbly bath.
"Rub-a-dub-dub, my bunny needs a scrub,"
she laughed. "Who's my beautiful baby?"
"I am!" said Little Bunny, smiling sweetly.

"Well now, darling, I think it's our bedtime,"
said Mrs Rabbit hopefully, drying his fur.

"No!" said Little Bunny. "Not bedtime yet."

Mrs Rabbit tried warm milk.

"Stirry, whirly, creamy white," she yawned.

"Time to cuddle and say goodnight."

Little Bunny reached up for a hug.

"Cuddle, yes! Not goodnight," he said.

He wanted to stay up with Mummy for ever.

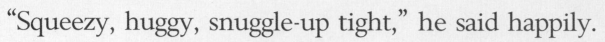

"Squeezy, huggy, snuggle-up tight," he said happily.
"Aren't I your best little bunny
in the world tonight?"

"I love all my babies the same,
sleepyhead," said Mrs Rabbit.

"Then I'll never be ready for bed,"
said Little Bunny.

"What am I to do with you?"
said his worn out mother.
Little Bunny jumped up excitedly . . .

"Let's play bunny hops!"
said Little Bunny.

"Hoppity, hoppity, hop,

round and round the
room till I . . ."

"Flop!" whispered
Mrs Rabbit.

"Zzzzzzz,"
went Little Bunny.

"Aaah, peace and quiet at last,"
sighed Mrs Rabbit.
"Even my youngest little bunny
is asleep in bed."

Mrs Rabbit fell into bed,
but through her snores
she heard . . .

...her second youngest bunny call,
"Mummy, I can't sleep!"